Pirican Pic and. Pirican Mor

Barefoot Books
3 Bow Street, 3rd Floor
Cambridge, MA 02138

This book was typeset in Ravie and Della Robbia, also Square 721, Benguiat, Marker Thin,
Grunge, VAG Rounded, Tahoma, Soupbone, Child's Play, HipHop and Goose. This book
is printed on 100% acid-free paper These illustrations were prepared in oil on Fabriano paper

Graphic design by Applecart, England
Color separation by Bright Arts Graphics, Singapore
Printed and bound in Singapore by Tien Wah Press (Pte) Ltd

Library of Congress Cataloging-in-Publication Data

Lupton, Hugh.
    Pirican Pic and Pirican Mor / retold by Hugh Lupton ; illustrated by Yumi Heo. —1st ed.
[40] p. : col. ill. ;   cm.
Summary: The story of two friends who go off to pick walnuts. Their adventure begins
after one friend has been busy picking the walnuts, while the other has eaten every one.
Based on a Scottish folktale.
ISBN 1-84148-070-3
1. Folklore — Scotland. I. Heo, Yumi. II. Title.
398.2/ 09411 21   2003

1 3 5 7 9 8 6 4 2

Pirican Pic
and
Pirican Mor

retold by Hugh Lupton

illustrated by Yumi Heo

Barefoot Books
Celebrating Art and Story

Once upon a time there lived two boys.
One was called Pirican Pic, the other was
called Pirican Mor.
One day they went to gather walnuts from
a walnut tree.
Pirican Mor climbed up among the branches
of the tree, picked the nuts and threw them
down to Pirican Pic.

Pirican Pic sat on the ground beneath
the branches of the tree, caught the
nuts as they came down, and cracked
them open with his little hammer.

But all the nuts that Pirican Pic cracked, he ate,
so that when Pirican Mor climbed down from the tree
there were no walnuts for him at all.
"Half those nuts were mine," he said. "I'm going to
find a stick and whack and thwack you for that."
So off went Pirican Mor in search of a stick.
Soon he found one, growing from the branch of a tree,
so he said to the tree:

"**I need a stick both hard and straight**
To **whack** and **thwack** poor Pirican Pic
Who ate **ALL** of my **WALNUTS!**"

"Well certainly, and of course," said
the tree, "but first you must find an
axe with which to cut me."

So off went Pirican Mor in search of an axe.
Soon he found one, lying beside a pile of wood chippings
on the floor of the forest, and so he said to the axe:

"I need an axe of heavy weight,
To cut the stick both hard and straight
To **whack** and **thwack** poor Pirican Pic
Who ate **ALL** of my **WALNUTS!"**

"By all means," said the axe, "but can't you see I'm blunt?
First you must find a sharpening stone with which to
grind me."

So off went Pirican Mor in search of a sharpening stone.
Soon he found one, lying among the pebbles beside the lake,
and so he said to the stone:

"I need a rough-edged sharpening stone,
To grind the axe of heavy weight,
To cut the stick both hard and straight
To **whack** and **thwack** poor Pirican Pic
Who ate **ALL** of my **WALNUTS!**"

"I'm yours for the using," said the sharpening stone,
"but first you must find some water with which to wet me."

So Pirican Mor knelt down by the wide blue
water of the lake and called out to it:

> "I need some water from the lake,
> To wet the rough-edged sharpening stone,
> To grind the axe of heavy weight,
> To cut the stick both hard and straight
> To **whack** and **thwack** poor Pirican Pic
> Who ate **ALL** of my **WALNUTS!**"

"Well and good," said the lake, "and you
can have as much of my water as you
like, but first you must find
a great-antlered stag
to swim across me."

So off went Pirican Mor in search of a stag.
Soon he found one, deep in the green thicket of
the forest, and so he said to the stag:

> "**I need a stag with antlers great,**
> **To swim across the lapping lake,**
> **To wet the rough-edged sharpening stone,**
> **To grind the axe of heavy weight,**
> **To cut the stick both hard and straight**
> **To whack and thwack poor Pirican Pic**
> **Who ate ALL of my WALNUTS!**"

"I will never swim the lake," said the stag, "unless you find
a fast-footed hunting dog to chase me to it."

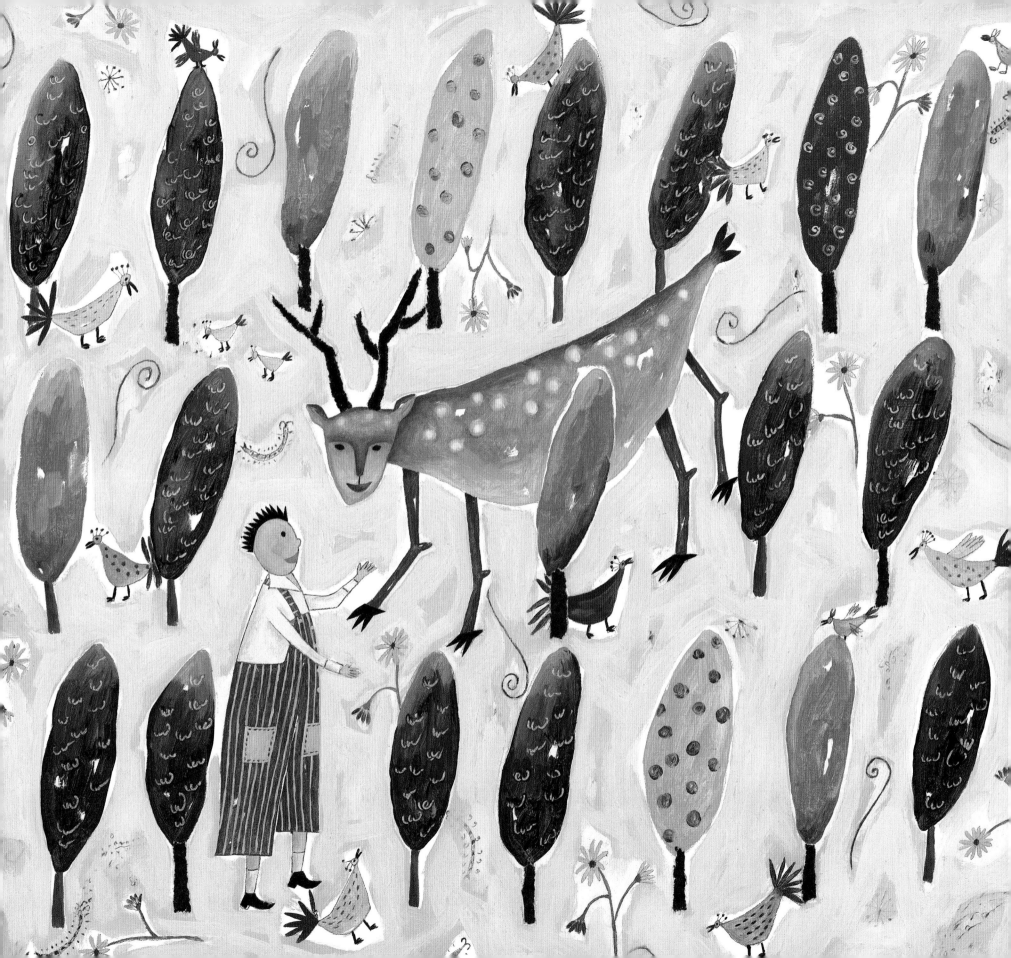

So off went Pirican Mor in search of a dog.
Soon he found one, curled up in a kennel, with ears pricked and
one eye open, and so he said to the dog:

"I need a dog both fast and fleet,
To chase the stag with antlers great,
To swim across the lapping lake,
To wet the rough-edged sharpening stone,
To grind the axe of heavy weight,
To cut the stick both hard and straight
To **whack** and **thwack** poor Pirican Pic
Who ate **ALL** of my **WALNUTS!**"

"Gladly will I chase the stag,"
said the dog, "but first you must rub
soft, yellow butter into my four feet."

So off went Pirican Mor in search of the butter.
Soon he found some, in a china dish on the farmhouse kitchen table,
and so he said to the butter:

"I need some butter soft and sweet,
To rub into the fast dog's feet,
To chase the stag with antlers great,
To swim across the lapping lake,
To wet the rough-edged sharpening stone,
To grind the axe of heavy weight,
To cut the stick both hard and straight
To **whack** and **thwack** poor Pirican Pic
Who ate **ALL** of my **WALNUTS!**"

"I'm yours for the taking," said the
butter, "but first you must find a
mouse to scrape me with its teeth."

Soon he found one, nibbling at the crumbs on the
farmhouse pantry floor, and so he said to the mouse:

"I need a mouse with nibbling teeth,
To scrape the butter soft and sweet,
To rub into the fast dog's feet,
To chase the stag with antlers great,
To swim across the lapping lake,
To wet the rough-edged sharpening stone,
To grind the axe of heavy weight,
To cut the stick both hard and straight
To **whack** and **thwack** poor Pirican Pic
Who ate **ALL** of my **WALNUTS!**"

"I will only scrape the butter," said the mouse,
"if you can find a fat, black cat to chase me to it."

So off went Pirican Mor in search of a cat.
Soon he found one, curled up and purring on
the warm tiles of the barn roof, and so he said:

"I need a cat as **black** as night,

To chase the mouse with nibbling teeth,

To scrape the butter soft and sweet,

To rub into the fast dog's feet,

To chase the stag with antlers great,

To swim across the lapping lake,

To wet the rough-edged sharpening stone,

To grind the axe of heavy weight,

To cut the stick both hard and straight

To **whack** and **thwack** poor Pirican Pic

Who ate **ALL** of my **WALNUTS!**"

"Chasing mice is my delight," said the cat, "but first,
bring me a saucerful of milk for I am thirsty."

So off went Pirican Mor in search of a cow.

Soon he found one, chewing slowly in the green meadow, and so he said:

"I need your creamy milk so white,
To give the cat as **black** as night,
To chase the mouse with nibbling teeth,
To scrape the butter soft and sweet,
To rub into the fast dog's feet,
To chase the stag with antlers great,
To swim across the lapping lake,
To wet the rough-edged sharpening stone,
To grind the axe of heavy weight,
To cut the stick both hard and straight
To **whack** and **thwack** poor Pirican Pic
Who ate **ALL** of my **WALNUTS!**"

"There's plenty of milk and more," said the cow, "and you can have as much as you like, but first bring me some corn from the barn."

So off went Pirican Mor in search of some corn. Soon he found the stable boy, sweeping the chaff from the floor of the barn, and so he said:

"I need some corn for the cow to eat,
To get the creamy milk so white,
To give the cat as **black** as night,
To chase the mouse with nibbling teeth,
To scrape the butter soft and sweet,
To rub into the fast dog's feet,
To chase the stag with antlers great,
To swim across the lapping lake,
To wet the rough-edged sharpening stone,
To grind the axe of heavy weight,
To cut the stick both hard and straight
To **whack** and **thwack** poor Pirican Pic
Who ate **ALL** of my **WALNUTS!"**

"There are stocks and stacks and sacks of corn to spare," said the stable boy, "but first you must run to the baker's shop and bring me a bun, warm from the oven."

So off went Pirican Mor to the baker's shop. And there was the baker, weighing flour into a great mixing bowl, and so he said:

"I need a bun for the boy to bite,
To get the corn for the cow to eat,
To get the creamy milk so white,
To give the cat as **black** as night,
To chase the mouse with nibbling teeth,
To scrape the butter soft and sweet,
To rub into the fast dog's feet,
To chase the stag with antlers great,
To swim across the lapping lake,
To wet the rough-edged sharpening stone,
To grind the axe of heavy weight,
To cut the stick both hard and straight
To **whack** and **thwack** poor Pirican Pic
Who ate **ALL** of my **WALNUTS!**"

"Cherry buns and currant buns and buns of every kind," said the baker, "but first I need some water to wet the flour to make the dough for the buns." And the baker gave Pirican Mor a sieve and told him to go to the well and fetch him some water.

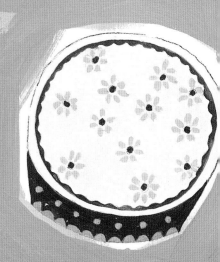

So off went Pirican Mor to the well, and he dipped the sieve into the water. But when he lifted the sieve, the water ran straight through the holes of it and back into the well. He tried again and the same thing happened.

Poor Pirican Mor!
He threw the sieve onto the ground, put his hands over his face and the hot tears came trickling down between his fingers.

Just then, high overhead, a great white seagull came flying by: "Rub soft black mud to it," the seagull cried, "rub soft black mud to it."

So Pirican Mor found some soft black mud, and he rubbed the mud into the sieve until all the holes were filled, and then he left the sieve in the sunshine, and when the mud was dry and hard he dipped the sieve into the well again. But the water washed the mud from the holes of the sieve, and it ran straight through and back into the well, just as it had before.
Poor Pirican Mor!

He threw the sieve onto the ground, put his hand over his face and the hot tears came trickling down between his fingers.
Just then, high overhead, a raggedy black crow came flying by:
"Rub sticky brown clay to it," the black crow cried, "rub sticky brown clay to it."

So Pirican Mor found some sticky brown clay, and he rubbed the clay into the holes of the sieve until all of them were filled, and he left the sieve in the sunshine.

And when the clay was dry and hard he dipped the sieve into the well again, and this time the clay stayed firm. And when Pirican Mor lifted the sieve from the well, there was not a trickle of water from it.

Carefully, without spilling a drop, Pirican Mor carried the water to the baker's shop. And the baker used the water to make the dough to bake the buns. And he gave Pirican Mor two of them, warm from the oven.

Well, Pirican Mor ate one of those buns,
but he gave the other to the stable boy,

Who gave him corn for the cow to eat,
Who gave him the creamy milk so white,
Which he gave to the cat as **black** as night,
Who chased the mouse with nibbling teeth,
Who scraped the butter soft and sweet,
which he rubbed into the fast dog's feet,
Who chased the stag with antlers great,
Who swam across the lapping lake,
Which wetted the rough-edged sharpening stone,
Which ground the axe of heavy weight,
Which cut the stick both hard and straight.
And Pirican Mor took the stick in his hand — now he'd
whack and he'd **thwack** poor Pirican Pic!

But when he came to the walnut tree
there was nobody there.
There was nobody there at all.

He looked this way and that way and all he could see was a pile of
walnuts, cracked and shelled, on the ground beneath the branches.
He picked one of them up and popped it into his mouth:
"Mmmmmm." He picked up another: "Delicious!" He threw his stick
into the bushes, sat down on the soft grass and…

ATE HIS WALNUTS!